DISCARD

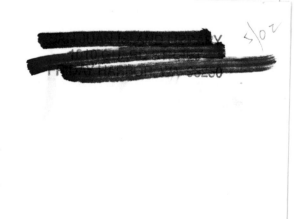

Dog Eared

For Françoise

A Doubleday Book for Young Readers
Published by
Random House Children's Books
a division of
Random House, Inc.
1540 Broadway
New York, New York 10036

DOUBLEDAY and the anchor with dolphin colophon are registered trademarks of
Random House, Inc.

Visit us on the Web! www.randomhouse.com/kids
Educators and librarians, for a variety of teaching tools, visit us at www.randomhouse.com/teachers

Library of Congress Cataloging-in-Publication Data
Harvey, Amanda.
   Dog Eared / written and illustrated by Amanda Harvey.
      p. cm.
   Summary: Self-conscious about its ears, a dog tries doing a number of things to make them look better.
   ISBN 0-385-72911-1 (trade)
          0-385-90845-8 (lib. bdg.)
   [1. Dogs—Fiction. 2. Ear—Fiction. 3. Self-acceptance—Fiction.] I. Title.
PZ7.H26745 Do 2001
[E]—dc21
                                                                                    00-059033

The text of this book is set in 19-point Truesdell.
Manufactured in the United States of America
March 2002
10 9 8 7 6 5 4 3 2 1

Dog Eared

Amanda Harvey

A Doubleday Book for Young Readers

I was walking home the other day

when a large dog pushed into me and growled,
"Out of my way, Big Ears!"

Big Ears? I thought. Surely not.
But doubt crept into my mind.

I stopped to look in a shop window.

My ears *were* quite large.

HUGE, in fact. How had I never noticed?

My appetite was gone. I couldn't eat any treats.

Or play with Max.

Or even chase the neighborhood cat.

I wanted to get home

and sort this ear problem out.

But that was easier said than done.
Should I gel them up?

Or curl them under?

Should I tie them in a bow?

Or wear them in a spiraling tower?

I didn't know. Nothing looked right.

What was I to do?

I went back downstairs
(eating some horrible peppermint creams along the way)

and went straight to bed.

But I had trouble falling asleep.

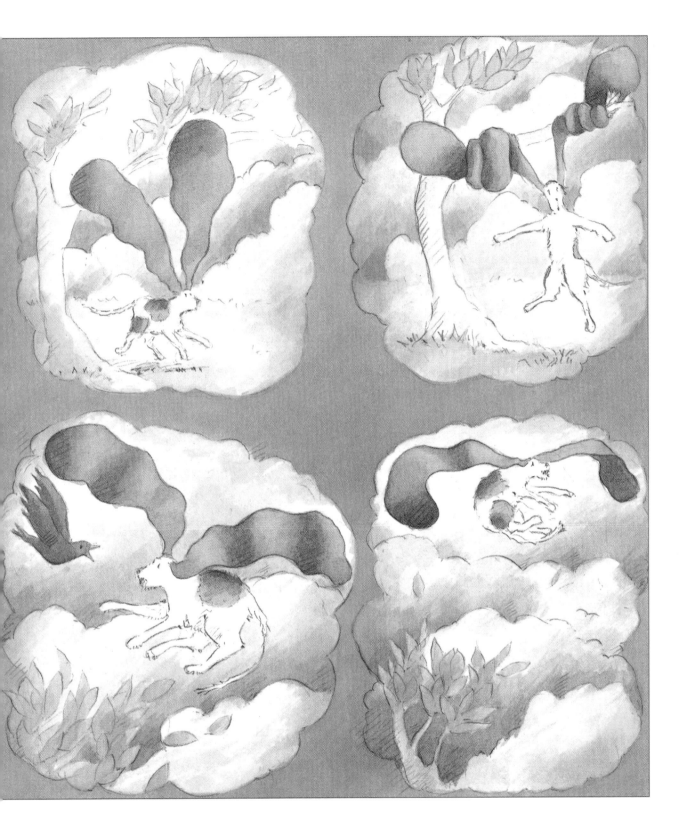

When I did, nightmares filled my thoughts.

In the dead of night, Lucy came in.
She snuggled next to me and wrapped one of my ears around her face.

"I love your large, silky, fabulous ears, Otis," she whispered,
and kissed the one that was keeping her warm. I sighed.

In the morning, I bounded out of bed
and ate a large breakfast.

Then I spent a busy day with Max in the park.

On the way home, that same dog pushed into me again
and said, "Out of my way, Fat Face!"

Fat Face?

I don't think so!